Rani

Two Friendship Tales

RANI AND THE THREE TREASURES

AND

RANI IN THE MERMAID LAGOON

RANDOM HOUSE 🏠 NEW YORK

ISBN: 978-0-7364-2730-2

www.randomhouse.com/kids

MANUFACTURED IN CHINA

10 9 8 7 6 5 4 3 2

All About Fairies

IF YOU HEAD toward the second star on your right and fly straight on till morning, you'll come to Never Land, a magical island where mermaids play and children never grow up.

When you arrive, you might hear something like the tinkling of little bells. Follow that sound and you'll find Pixie Hollow, the secret heart of Never Land.

A great old maple tree grows in Pixie

Hollow, and in it live hundreds of fairies and sparrow men. Some of them can do water magic, others can fly like the wind, and still others can speak to animals. You see, Pixie Hollow is the Never fairies' kingdom, and each fairy who lives there has a special, extraordinary talent.

Not far from the Home Tree, nestled in the branches of a hawthorn, is Mother Dove, the most magical creature of all. She sits on her egg, watching over the fairies, who in turn watch over her. For as long as Mother Dove's egg stays well and whole, no one in Never Land will ever grow old.

Once, Mother Dove's egg *was* broken. But we are not telling the story of the egg here. Now it is time for Rani's tales. . . .

Rani
and the
Three
Treasures

Rani
and the
Three
Treasures

WRITTEN BY
KIMBERLY MORRIS

ILLUSTRATED BY
THE DISNEY STORYBOOK ARTISTS

RANDOM HOUSE 🏠 NEW YORK

1

"OH, NO!"

Prilla held up her hand and let the water splash into her palm. "Rain! The day is ruined. Hurry, let's get back to the Home Tree before my wings get wet." She fanned her wings and began to lift off from the ground.

Rani took Prilla's hand and tugged her back. "Don't be silly," she said with a laugh. "Rainy days are just as much fun as sunny days."

Prilla frowned. "I don't see how. If your wings get wet, you can't fly. And if you can't fly, then . . ." Prilla broke off. "Oh, Rani. I'd fly backward if I could. I forgot."

"Don't worry." Rani smiled. She knew her friend Prilla would never hurt her feelings on purpose. All fairies loved to fly. Rani was the only fairy in Pixie Hollow who couldn't. But Rani wasn't unhappy. She was too full of life.

The rain began to fall faster. Prilla covered her face. She flinched as each heavy drop struck her.

But Rani was a water-talent fairy. To her, every raindrop felt like a kiss. Rani loved the water, and the water loved her.

"Watch this, Prilla!" Rani ran as fast as she could toward a puddle. She skidded into the puddle, and the water formed a geyser that lifted her up as if she were on a pedestal. It twirled her around. "Wheee!" Rani cried.

Prilla clapped her hands. "Rani! Can you make it do that for me?"

"Sure! Come on in," she urged.

Prilla lowered her head and ran splashing into the puddle, just as she had seen Rani do. Rani stretched her arms out to the water. It moved toward her like iron to a magnet. She threw her arms up like a conductor signaling an orchestra.

Voilà! The water created a second

geyser that lifted Prilla into the air until she was level with Rani.

Rani laughed. "Now let's seesaw!" The twin water pedestals began to move. Up and down. Up and down. Prilla up. Rani down. Rani up. Prilla down.

Soon both the fairies were laughing so hard, they were in danger of falling off their water pedestals. "Water down," Rani commanded, lowering her arms.

The twin geysers gently subsided. Rani looked down at a shallow puddle spreading out before her feet. She leaned over and grasped the edges of the puddle with her hands. Then she pulled up a sheet of water as if it were a bolt of silvery silk.

She wrapped it around herself like

a shimmering cloak. The water gleamed and glittered. It reflected the trees, the sky, and the astonished sparkle in Prilla's eyes.

"How beautiful!" Prilla gasped. "You look like a queen."

Rani held out her hands and quickly caught a raindrop. She held her hands over Prilla's head and let it drip through her fingers. Each droplet was like a tiny diamond. The drops stacked up on Prilla's head and formed a glittering water tiara.

"Now you need a dress to go with that tiara. Water sequins, I think." Rani pulled off her water cape and twirled it in the air. The silky sheet of water broke into a thousand silvery drops. They

rained back down on Prilla, clinging to her arms, legs, and torso. Within seconds, Prilla was covered in a sparkling gown of water sequins, complete with a long train.

Prilla took a hesitant step. She expected the watery gown and crown to immediately drip away. But when she moved, they moved with her.

"Rani, you are amazing!" said Prilla. "No wonder you love the water. Believe it or not, I hope it rains again—"

"—tomorrow?" Rani said with a laugh. She had a habit of finishing her friends' sentences for them. "I wish that every day. But rain is rare in Pixie Hollow."

"Wouldn't it be wonderful if you could make it rain whenever—"

"—I wanted? Yes! I can't imagine anything more fun." Rani turned her face up and watched the clouds drift away. It *would* be wonderful to make it rain whenever she wanted. In fact, Rani had been thinking about that for a long time.

Just then, Rani saw a small rain

cloud trailing behind the other clouds. Its fluffy edges gleamed silver against the late afternoon sun.

If Rani wanted her own personal rain cloud, that little cloud would be the perfect one. Rani pressed her lips together, thinking.

"I'm getting cold," Prilla said. She shook off her watery finery. "I'm going inside to dry off. I'll see you—"

"—later." Rani waved as Prilla walked back to the Home Tree, where the fairies lived.

Prilla was the only mainland-visiting clapping-talent fairy in Pixie Hollow. In a blink, she could transport herself to the mainland where Clumsies—that is, humans—lived and urge them to clap to show they believed in fairies.

Everyone in Pixie Hollow had been amazed and surprised to discover that Prilla had such an unusual talent. But after a very short time, they stopped being amazed and surprised and took it very much for granted. After all, why *wouldn't* a fairy have an unusual talent?

Never Land was an amazing and surprising place with more kinds of magic than anyone could ever understand or imagine. But it was their talents that made the fairies so special. A talent was a kind of magic. And Rani's water talent seemed to be getting stronger and stronger every day. Her relationship to water, and all things made from it, was becoming more personal.

Maybe it was because she couldn't fly. Maybe Rani took all the passion that the other fairies devoted to their flying and devoted it instead to her talent.

Rani watched the clouds disappear into the distance. The smallest one with the gleaming edges trailed behind. There was something Rani had wanted to try for a long time. Something that would test the power of her talent.

Now, Rani decided boldly. *Now is the time!*

2

Rani raced up the spiral stairs inside the trunk of the Home Tree. She ran down the hallway. Her room was located at the very end of one of the longest branches.

Once she was in her room, Rani hurried to the window. She parted the seaweed curtains and peered out.

Rani's room was always damp,

which was exactly how she liked it. A permanent leak in the ceiling dripped into a tub made from a human-sized thimble. A Never minnow swam happily in the tub.

Rani listened hard as the water splashed into the thimble. Water spoke a magic language full of dots, plops, plinks, and gurgles. Rani felt as if the water were speaking directly to her. She could hear it encouraging her. It was telling her exactly how to coax the little gray rain cloud back to Pixie Hollow.

Rani fixed her gaze on the cloud and leaned out the window as far as she dared. She stretched out her arms and began to imitate the sounds of the dots, plops, plinks, and gurgles. She called out to the cloud, speaking the language of water.

The little cloud with the shining silver silhouette seemed to pause. Then, drawn by the sound of Rani's voice, it began to move toward her. While the rest of the clouds moved on, little by little the small cloud came drifting back toward the Home Tree.

Rani put every drop of her strength into her water spell. Finally, the cloud hovered right over the branch of the Home Tree where Rani's room was perched.

Exhausted, Rani sank back onto her bed. She listened to the rain patter on the ground outside. She felt the gray watery mist of the cloud come in through the window. It surrounded her like a soft, moist blanket. Her eyelids fluttered, and she fell asleep.

Rani awoke with a start. The sun shone on her face. She found herself looking out the window at a clear blue sky.

"Why! I fell asleep in my clothes," she said.

She pulled the seaweed curtain aside and looked out at the sunny day. There wasn't a rain cloud in sight.

Rani realized that she had been dreaming. She couldn't help feeling disappointed. Having her own little rain cloud would have been wonderful.

She hurried downstairs. As she

stepped outside to look for Brother Dove, she heard someone call to her.

"Yoo-hoo! Rani!"

Rani looked up. She saw Prilla waving from the window of her own room in the Home Tree.

Prilla flew out the window and landed lightly on the ground beside Rani. "I had such a good time playing in the rain yesterday. I was almost disappointed when I woke up and saw—"

"—the sun?" Rani finished for her. "Me, too. In fact, you'll laugh when I tell you what I dreamed."

Rani told Prilla all about her dream. Prilla giggled at the idea of Rani having a cloud of her own. "What a shame it turned out to be a dream," she said.

"But don't be too disappointed. Sunny days might not be as much fun as rainy days, but they're good for getting things done. What shall we do today?"

As they stood chatting in the soft, yellow morning sunlight, a shadow slowly moved overhead. It blocked out

the sun. Moments later, a raindrop splashed down next to them.

Rani looked up and drew in her breath. Hovering overhead was a small gray cloud.

"Prilla! It's the cloud from my dream!" Rani exclaimed.

"It can't be," Prilla said.

"It is!" Rani argued. "I know it. I feel it. It's my very own cloud. Oh, Prilla! It wasn't a dream. I am so lucky!"

Suddenly, Rani heard an odd sound. It sounded like laughter. But it also sounded like water moving through a pipe. "Did you hear that noise?" she asked Prilla.

"I heard a gurgling sound," Prilla replied.

Rani looked down and saw water collecting in a hole next to a root. The water bounced around in the hollow, bubbling and frothing. "I guess that's what we heard." She turned her face up and spread her arms, welcoming the rain. "Just think," she said to Prilla. "Now I can take a walk in the rain every single day, and nobody else has to get wet."

Prilla flew a few feet to the side so she was out of the cloud's shadow. The drizzle fell only on Rani. Prilla laughed. "How perfect. Come on, let's walk to Havendish Stream and see if it follows."

The two fairies began walking toward the stream. All the while, the little rain cloud hovered over Rani and showered her. Some drops plopped on her head, as if the cloud were teasing her and trying to get her to join in a game. Rani broke into a run, trying to escape the drops. The little cloud chased her. It pounded the top of her head with water. Finally, she gave up and slowed down.

Soon Rani and Prilla were laughing so hard they could hardly move. Once again, Rani heard the sound of strange laughter. This time it sounded like water rushing out of a faucet into a copper pot.

Rani began to get an odd feeling. Someone—or *something*—was watching them. But who? What?

Then suddenly, out of the corner of

her eye, Rani saw a figure zip from one flower to another.

Rani pretended not to see. And she didn't say anything to Prilla. She was already planning a way to catch the spy.

"Come on, Prilla," she said in a loud voice. "I'll race you to Havendish Stream." Rani broke into a run. Prilla chased behind her, flying a few inches overhead. Then, without warning, Rani came to a sudden stop and whirled around.

Prilla shot past her. "Hey!" she cried out in surprise.

Rani kept her eyes focused on one spot. Whoever it was, or whatever it was, froze. It stood perfectly still, hoping to blend into the background.

But Rani's eyes were keen. "I see you," she said.

Rani heard a mischievous giggle. It sounded like a bucket splashing down into a well. "If you can see me, I guess there's no point in hiding," the strange creature said. It stepped forward.

Prilla flew over and landed on the ground next to Rani. "What is it?" Prilla whispered.

It *looked* like a fairy, but it wasn't. For one thing, it had no wings. In fact, it had no body either. It was a transparent, shimmering figure made of clear water. When it stood still, it was almost invisible. But when it moved, its watery form reflected the sky, the trees, and the flowers.

Rani stared at the remarkable creature. "Who are you? And why are you following us?"

The watery figure laughed. The noise sounded like water splashing in a fountain.

"My name is Dab," the creature said. "I'm a water sprite. *And that's my cloud.*"

3

"*Your* cloud!" Rani cried.

Dab nodded. "Yes. My cloud."

Rani was horrified. "Oh, dear. I didn't know it belonged to anyone. You can have it back. I would never have called it to me if I had known."

Dab laughed. It sounded like water swirling around a rock in a stream. "I've been following you," she said. "I wanted to see what kind of a cloud keeper you would be. You really have a way with rain clouds." Dab wicked this way and that, reflecting colors like a prism. "Clouds are sensitive creatures. You must be a very special water creature yourself."

Rani blushed with pleasure. "Well, I am a water-talent fairy. That's why I was able to call the cloud. I guess it's also why I could see you when you were standing still." She sighed. "I'll miss having my own cloud. It is such a treasure. I can't help feeling envious."

Dab shimmered. "Surely you fairies have treasures of your own?"

Rani laughed. "Oh, yes. Of course. But nothing as wonderful as a rain cloud."

"Maybe you would like to look after the cloud for me?" Dab suggested.

"You mean the cloud could stay?" Prilla asked, her eyes wide. She turned to Rani. "Wouldn't that be fantastic?"

Dab chuckled. It sounded like water pouring from a watering can. "Would you promise to be a good cloud keeper?" she asked Rani.

"Of course," Rani replied.

"Promise on your talent," Dab challenged.

"I promise on my talent," Rani said promptly.

Dab smiled and shimmered. "Good! I now pronounce you the official cloud keeper. But there are a couple of things you should know. Clouds need a lot of attention. Someone must lead them and watch over them. Otherwise, they get nervous and fidgety. If they get riled up, they make a tremendous ruckus. Thunder. Lightning. Wind. Sleet. Hail. Even the little ones like that"—she pointed her transparent thumb toward the sky—"will make trouble if they get upset."

In the distance, Rani saw something in the sky. Lots of great, big, fat, fluffy, gray rain clouds moving in her direction.

"Ummm . . ." Rani pointed to the sky. "What are those?"

"The rest of my clouds," said Dab.

"Why are they coming this way?" Rani asked.

"Because you're the official cloud

keeper now," Dab replied. "From now on, wherever *you* go, *they* go."

"I can't keep them *all!*" Rani cried.

Dab chuckled. "You have to. You promised. You promised on your talent."

"But . . . but . . . I thought I was promising to keep *one*. One small one."

"Where one goes, the others follow," Dab explained.

"You didn't tell me that," Rani protested angrily.

"You didn't ask."

"You tricked me," Rani accused.

Dab laughed. It sounded like water hammering on a tin roof. "Yes, I did. I've been keeping watch over those clouds for the longest time. I'll be glad to have a holiday."

"A holiday? What kind of a holiday?"

"I'd like to see Never Land in the sunshine. When you travel with rain clouds, you never really get a good sense of the scenery. So I thought I would do a little sightseeing."

By now the entire sky was filled with dark gray clouds. A heavy rain began to fall. Rani had to shout to be heard over it. "But when will you be back?"

Dab laughed. "That depends on you."

"Me?"

Dab nodded. "You told me you have no treasure as wonderful as a rain cloud. But actually, the fairies of Pixie Hollow have three wonderful treasures—treasures that everyone would envy and want to possess. When you guess what those three treasures are, you must name them out loud and then say, '*I wish you back! I wish you back! I wish you back!*' Until then . . . you're in charge."

And with that, Dab disappeared into the air.

It was a long, wet walk back to the Home Tree. Prilla's wings were so heavy with rain she couldn't get off the ground— not even with double sprinkles of fairy dust.

Rani looked up at the sky. The gray clouds hovered overhead. Sometimes they dropped gentle rain. Sometimes

they dropped heavy rain. And sometimes they just contented themselves
with being damp.

"What are we going to do now?"
Prilla asked.

Rani noticed that Prilla had asked
what are *we* going to do, and not what
are *you* going to do. She felt grateful

that her friend wanted to help her.

"Well," Rani said, "I must say, I don't think Dab's riddle is very challenging. Pixie Hollow has lots of treasures. It shouldn't take us long to guess them. Mother Dove's egg is one." Mother Dove's egg was what kept the creatures in Never Land from growing old.

"What about Queen Clarion's crown?" Prilla suggested.

"Yes! That's two. Maybe Mother Dove is the third. Let's see if we're right." Rani lifted her voice. "Hear me, Dab, wherever you are. In the name of Pixie Hollow's three treasures—the blue egg, Mother Dove, and Queen Clarion's crown—I wish you back . . . I wish you back . . . I wish you back!"

Rani and Prilla stood very still, waiting for Dab to appear.

But nothing happened except that a big, fat raindrop fell and splashed on Rani's head. "Okay," she chirped, refusing to worry. "It may be a little harder than I thought."

"We will figure it out," Prilla said.

In spite of the chilly rain, a wave of happiness warmed Rani from head to toe. She was glad Prilla was such a good friend.

4

Two DAYS LATER, it was still raining. As Rani sat drinking tea, she couldn't help noticing that the tearoom was full of glum fairies.

Rani reached out and took a crumpet from the breadbasket. The crumpet bent slightly, then broke off. It landed with a *plop* right in her cup of tea.

Dulcie, who had baked the crumpets,

sighed impatiently. "Every single piece of pastry is soggy. And there's nothing we can do about it with the weather so damp."

A laundry-talent fairy folded her arms over her chest. "We've got piles and piles of wet laundry. But we can't hang it out to dry until the rain stops."

"I don't understand it," said Iridessa, a light-talent fairy. "Usually Pixie Hollow only gets as much rain as it needs. But we've had a good bit more than we need. In fact, we're having too much. The roots of the Home Tree are so wet the fairies on the first floor are complaining of rising damp."

Rani said nothing. The first day of rain had been fun—at least for her and

Prilla. The other fairies had seemed to enjoy the rainy day, too. Many had spent the time reading, chatting, and tidying their work spaces.

But by the end of the second day, the mood had worsened. In the kitchen, the cooking- and baking-talent fairies exchanged harsh words. The light-talent fairies were exhausted from trying to keep the hallways and workplaces lit. And the coiffure talents had given up in despair. In this kind of weather, they said, curls were impossible to tame. So they hung up a sign that read FAIRIES EXPERIENCING BAD HAIR ARE ADVISED TO WEAR A HAT UNTIL FURTHER NOTICE.

Rani listened to the unhappy voices. If the other fairies ever found out that

it was her fault the rain clouds were hanging around, it would be awful.

Prilla entered the tearoom and made her way over to Rani. "Any ideas?" she whispered.

Rani sighed. She had been racking her brains all night.

Kyto the dragon had a collection of

rare objects far more priceless than anything in Pixie Hollow. Hook had chests full of pirate bounty, and the mermaids had the lovely treasures of the sea. What treasures did the fairies have that none of the others did?

Rani thought about her wings. She had asked Prilla to cut them off so she could swim in the ocean with the mermaids. It had been part of the quest to save Mother Dove and her blue egg.

As soon as she'd cut her wings off, they'd turned into tiny jeweled marvels. Those wings—those *treasures*—had helped to save Never Land. Rani had given them to Kyto in exchange for his help.

Rani had never regretted giving away

her wings—until now. Maybe the wings were one of the treasures Dab described.

Rani shook her head. No, that couldn't be it. Her wings weren't part of Pixie Hollow. They belonged to Kyto now.

It was clear to Rani that she and Prilla would have to go on a treasure hunt. But in the meantime, maybe there was a short-term solution.

Rani went outside and whistled for Brother Dove. He swooped down from a nearby branch. *Poor thing*, Rani thought. He was wet from head to toe.

"Maybe we can create a little dry time for Pixie Hollow," Rani told Brother Dove. "The clouds will follow where we lead. So let's head for the caves and see if we can lose them there."

Brother Dove took to the sky and headed north. Rani looked behind her. Sure enough, here came the flock of gray rain clouds. They trailed at a distance, but they moved with steady purpose.

Rani indicated to Brother Dove that he should change direction. Brother Dove flew below the rain clouds and headed the opposite way.

"Faster," Rani urged. Brother Dove beat his wings harder.

Rani looked back and saw the clouds swiftly reverse their direction. They were determined to follow.

Then Rani spotted a cave in the side

of a hill. "Let's hide and see what happens. Maybe they'll just drift away and find Dab on their own," she said.

Brother Dove dropped his altitude and soared below the hilltop. He circled once and then ducked into the mouth of a hidden cave.

Inside the cave, they waited. Rani peered out of the entrance at the sky. She could see the clouds, but she was hidden from them. The fluffy rain clouds began to mill around, bumping into one another like anxious, agitated sheep. They moved uncertainly this way and that. Within minutes, they were a tangled, roiling gray mass.

Thunder began to echo through the valley. It grew louder and louder, reverberating through the cave. Jagged lightning flashed. Rain poured down in sheets.

Rani peered out of the cave. The wind whipped her long hair in every direction. She grabbed on to a blade of grass to keep from blowing away.

This was terrible. She couldn't let it go on. If the clouds didn't calm down, they might cause another hurricane. *Besides,* Rani thought guiltily, *I promised I would be a good cloud keeper.* She had to honor that promise.

"Let's go," she told Brother Dove. He whisked her out of the cave. "Fly toward the rain clouds," she said. "But slowly. We don't want to spook them."

Brother Dove flew gently into the

fluffy mass of clouds. The cloudy air was cold and wet on Rani's cheeks. Tiny bits of ice grazed her skin.

"I'm here," Rani said in a soothing voice. "I'm here. Everything is going to be fine." She reached out her hand to pat one of the clouds. Her hand sank into nothingness. But the clouds seemed to sense her presence. They calmed down.

"Come on," she said. "Let's go home."

The thunder began to die out. The lightning faded away. The hurling sheets of rain slowed to a light patter. Rani and Brother Dove flew back toward Pixie Hollow, the flock of rain clouds following behind them.

As they approached the Home Tree,

Rani could see lots of fairies busy out-side. They were gardening, dancing, and hanging laundry out to dry.

They were not going to be happy to see the rain return. Nope. They were not going to be happy at all.

5

RANI LOOKED AT each and every one of the
shells in her collection. Were there any
treasures among them? Treasures that
everyone would envy and want to possess?

Rani held her conch shell to her ear.
She listened to the sound of the ocean.
This shell was a treasure, but only to her.
It had been a gift from the water fairy
Silvermist. It was the first gift Rani had

received when she arrived in Never
Land.

There was a knock on the door, and
Rani hurried to open it. Prilla stood on
her doorstep. She wore a rain hat and a
slicker made from a lily pad, and she carried a petal umbrella. Despite the fact
that she was as cold and damp as the
other fairies, Prilla had a big smile on her
face. "Ready to search for treasure?"

"I'm ready," Rani replied. "First stop,
Aiden's crown repair shop. If there are any
rare or precious jewels in Pixie Hollow,
that will be the place to find them."

Aiden, the crown-repair sparrow man,
was delighted to see Rani and Prilla.

"Visitors! To what do I owe the pleasure?"

"We're taking inventory," Rani said quickly. "We're counting all of Pixie Hollow's treasures. Aside from Queen Clarion's crown, do you know of any extraspecial jewels?"

Aiden rubbed his hands together. "You bet I do. Take a look at these." He reached for a wooden box and turned it upside down. Beautiful gemstones fell onto the table. They twinkled in the light.

Prilla gasped. "Oh, my! They are beautiful. Are they treasures?"

"Yes, of course," Aiden said. "Look at that moonstone. It used to be the centerpiece of Queen Clarion's crown."

Rani reached down and picked up the moonstone. A tiny vein ran across it. "Is that a crack?" she asked.

Aiden nodded. "Yes, a wonderful crack. One day, Tink and Beck were flying with the queen when a hawk came swooping down from out of nowhere."

Prilla gasped. "They could have been killed!"

"That's right," Aiden said. "But quick as lightning, Tink grabbed the crown from Queen Clarion's head. She took that dagger she always wears and pried this big moonstone right out of the crown. Then she tossed the moonstone to Beck. Beck loaded it into her slingshot and—*pow!* She got that old hawk right on his beak."

Rani and Prilla applauded.

"That hawk flew away and never came back. But the impact cracked the moonstone. Queen Clarion said never to fix it. That crack makes the moonstone priceless."

Aiden showed them every jewel in his workshop. He had a story to go with each one. It was almost an hour before Rani and Prilla left the crown-repair shop.

As they stepped outside, Prilla raised her umbrella. Her eyes were bright.

"Well? What do you think?" she asked breathlessly. "Did we find three treasures? Do you want to name them and wish Dab back?"

Rani sighed and shook her head.

"Remember all the things we saw on our quest? Hook has bigger and finer jewels on his watch fob alone. Compared to his jewels, ours look like . . . well, pea gravel."

Prilla's face fell.

"All those jewels are treasures, but only to us. They're treasures because of their history. But they're not treasures that everyone would envy or want to possess," Rani explained.

Prilla snapped her fingers. "I know! What about the pearls in the fountain? The beautiful pearls you brought from the Mermaid Lagoon."

Again, Rani shook her head. "Those pearls are nothing compared to the ones the mermaids wear. Their pearls are ten times the size of any pearl in Pixie Hollow."

"All right then," Prilla said. "Let's go look at some art. Maybe we'll find a treasure or two in Bess's studio."

As they approached her studio, Rani and Prilla could hear Bess humming. They knocked on the door. Bess answered with a paintbrush in her hand.

When she saw Rani and Prilla, she grinned. "I'm so glad someone's come by. I have a new masterpiece to show."

"Is it a treasure?" Prilla blurted out.

Bess laughed. "Terence would think so." She stepped back and picked up a piece of sea glass on which she had painted a portrait of Tinker Bell. Light streaming through the sea glass made the painting glow.

Prilla clapped her hands in delight. "How beautiful!"

"Yes," Bess said. "I'm glad I had this nice piece of sea glass to practice on.

Because—" Bess broke off. "Can you keep a secret?"

Rani and Prilla nodded.

"I have something wonderful. Something that will make everyone's eyes pop," Bess told them.

Prilla and Rani looked at each other. "Would you call it a treasure?" Prilla asked.

"Oh, *yes*. Look at this." Bess went to the corner where something very large was covered with a cloth. She removed the cloth with a flourish to reveal an enormous piece of sea glass. It was almost as big as Bess. "I'm going to paint a portrait of Mother Dove on it."

Rani's mouth fell open in amazement. "That piece of sea glass is huge.

How did you carry it all the way from the beach?"

"Terence gave me a bit of extra fairy dust in exchange for painting that picture of Tink." Bess quickly covered the sea glass with the cloth. "Don't tell a soul about this," she begged. "I want it to be a surprise."

Rani and Prilla promised they would keep her secret.

Outside the studio, Prilla looked at Rani expectantly. "Well? What do you think?"

"It's a lovely piece of sea glass," Rani told her. "But I've seen pieces of sea glass much bigger and smoother."

Prilla's normally friendly face darkened. "Why are you being so discouraging about all of the treasures in Pixie Hollow?"

"I'm not!" Rani cried.

"Yes, you are," Prilla fumed. "You know what? I think you don't *want* to find Pixie Hollow's treasures. Because deep down you really want the rain to stay forever, even though it's making the rest of us miserable." And with that, Prilla burst into tears.

Rani felt tears forming in her own eyes. "Oh, no! Prilla! Why would you say such a thing? You must know that's not true."

Prilla cried harder. She pulled a leaf-kerchief from her pocket and dabbed at her eyes. "You're right. I *do* know it's not true. I don't have any idea why I said it."

"I know why you said it. You said it because the rain is making you cranky and sad, just like it's making everybody cranky and sad."

Rani handed Prilla her own leafkerchief, which wasn't much help. Rani's leafkerchiefs were always damp. She patted Prilla on the shoulder. "There, there," she said in a soothing tone. "There, there."

Then suddenly, Rani spied something. She pointed at it, so excited that all she could manage to say was, *"There! There!"*

IN THE DISTANCE, Rani spied a beautiful rainbow.

"That's it!" Prilla said happily. "There's always a treasure at the end of a rainbow. Maybe there's a treasure in Pixie Hollow we don't know about."

Rani nodded. "Brother Dove can fly to the top of the rainbow. We can follow it all the way to the end."

She whistled, and Brother Dove swooped down from a nearby branch. Rani hopped on his back. "Wish me luck, Prilla."

Brother Dove spread his wings. They flew high up into the clouds. All of Never Land spread out below them—the forests, the shores, the lakes, the streams, and the villages. It was magnificent.

It might be lonely being the only fairy with no wings, Rani reflected. *But I wouldn't trade places with anybody.* She might not have any wings, but no fairy could fly higher.

Up . . . up . . . up they went. They were heading for the rainbow's arch. Finally, they reached the place where white light bent in the mist and reflected all the colors. It was the highest point of the rainbow.

Brother Dove was breathing hard. His wings were losing strength. Luckily, he wouldn't have to fly any higher. Now they could glide back to the ground.

Brother Dove arced in the air. He began to follow the rainbow's curve back toward the ground.

Faster and faster they went. The ground seemed to rush toward them. Rani looked down and saw the roof of the fairy-dust mill.

"Aiiiiiieeee!" she screamed.

As Brother Dove slowed, Rani pitched forward off his back. *BANG!* She fell right on top of the thatched roof. The thick straw cushioned her fall, but it was wet. Rani felt the roof give way beneath her.

CRASH! Rani fell through the roof. She landed with a *pooof!* right in the middle of a bin full of fairy dust. She flailed and struggled in the dust. Finally, Terence and Jerome leaned over the

side of the bin and hauled her out.

Rani blinked her eyes, shaking the dust from her eyelashes. She saw the light fairies Fira, Iridessa, and Luna. They stood with their hands on their hips, glaring at her. Nearby, Glory and Helios, two young light-talent fairies, burst into a fit of giggles.

But the other light fairies didn't seem amused at all. And Terence and Jerome looked perfectly horrified.

"Rani, what in Never Land are you doing?" Terence asked.

Rani had never been so embarrassed. "Well . . . I . . . um . . . saw the rainbow. And I thought I'd try to find out what was at the end of it."

Fira shook her head. "*We're* at the

end of it. We light talents made the rainbow. And now you've ruined our work."

"We've been using light to try to keep the dust dry," Iridessa explained. "When our light mingled with the rain, it created a rainbow."

Rain began dripping through the hole in the roof. Drops splashed into the bin of fairy dust.

"Oh, no!" Jerome shouted. "You've punched a hole in the roof and now the dust is going to get drenched. As if we weren't having enough trouble keeping it dry already."

"Now, now," Terence said. "There's no time for blaming. Quick, get some oilcloth and cover the bins."

Everyone sprang into action.

"Can I help?" Rani asked.

"I think you've done enough already," Fira snapped.

Rani felt her face flush hot and then cold with humiliation and regret. "Then I'll just, um . . . just . . ."

She couldn't finish. She ran outside, determined not to cause any more trouble.

But the moment she stepped outside the mill, a gust of wind hit her. It carried her up into the air.

"Help!" Rani cried. "Help!"

The fairy dust that covered her like flour had made her so buoyant she floated. The tiniest puff of wind sent her tossing and turning through the sky like a leaf.

Rani had no wings, so she had no way to control her movements. She tumbled and rolled through the air, going higher and higher. Soon she was lost in the thick fog of the clouds.

Tears ran down Rani's face. She had ruined everything. First, she had brought rain to Pixie Hollow. And now it looked as if she had spoiled Pixie Hollow's supply of fairy dust.

Another gust of wind sent her tumbling. She moved through the sky with the clouds. *Maybe this was the best thing that could have happened*, she thought miserably. *Maybe the clouds and I should blow away for good. Then Pixie Hollow can return to normal.*

Rani thought the other fairies were

probably *glad* she had blown away. They would be relieved to be rid of such a troublemaker. And they would be especially happy to be rid of the neverending rain.

Rani realized that none of those things were really true, but she couldn't help thinking them anyway. She felt miserable.

She began to sob. She was crying so loudly, she almost didn't hear her name.

"Raniiiiii? Raniiiii? Where are youuuuuuuu?"

Rani blinked her tears away. She peered through the foggy mist of the clouds. She couldn't believe her eyes. Here came Brother Dove with Prilla and

Fira on his back. The two fairies carried long ropes of woven lemongrass looped over their shoulders.

Prilla unwound one of the ropes. "Tie one end around your belt, so we can take you down," she told Rani.

She tossed the end of the rope to Rani. Rani reached out. But the motion sent her turning over and over.

"Try again!" Fira urged.

They tossed the rope once more. This time, Rani managed to grab it. She tied the end to her belt. "I can't believe it. I thought you were going to leave me up here," she said.

Fira yelped, "Leave you up in the air? Rani! What are you thinking? Of course we wouldn't leave you."

Brother Dove, Prilla, and Fira carefully towed her through the air, back to Pixie Hollow. As they approached the ground, Rani saw that several fairies had gathered. They peered up at Rani with worried faces. Queen Clarion was at the very front. Her helper fairies held broad petal umbrellas over her to keep her dry.

Fresh tears rolled down Rani's cheeks. But this time, they were tears of happiness. The fairies were all concerned about Rani. Despite the rain, they all had come to make sure she was okay.

As soon as Rani's feet touched the ground, the fairies began to applaud. Rani knew she owed them the truth. She held up her hands and took a deep breath. "I'm safe and sound. And I have something to tell you all. . . ."

Rani told Queen Clarion and the rest of the fairies the whole story of how she came to have the clouds and why they wouldn't leave.

When she was done, there was a long silence. Rani wondered what would happen next. Would Queen Clarion scold her? Banish her? Blame her for everything that had gone wrong?

Instead, Queen Clarion turned to the rest of the fairies and spoke in a clear, strong voice. "Fairies! You have all heard Rani. I know water sprites. They are mischievous, but they are not wicked. Dab will come back and take these clouds away. But she has posed a riddle and we must solve it."

The queen waved her arms. "Let us all work together. Go to your rooms. Go to your workshops. Go to your studios. Look in your special hiding places. I want every talent group to bring their treasures to the fairy circle. We have so many treasures! Surely we can find three that everyone would envy and want to possess."

7

THE CARPENTER-TALENT fairies quickly
raised tent poles in the fairy circle. The
weaving-talent fairies brought their
sturdiest cloth. Soon, a large canopy
covered the entire clearing, protecting it
from the rain.

Within an hour of Queen Clarion's
announcement, the fairies and sparrow
men began to arrive. They displayed

their treasures on tables set up beneath the canopy.

Rani had never seen so many wonderful things in one place. The coiffure-talent fairies showed off hair ornaments and combs made from gold and pewter. The garden-talent fairies piled their table high with beautiful flowers and mouthwatering fruit. The table-setting-talent fairies brought out dishes made from porcelain as thin as paper.

"My goodness," Rani said to Prilla as they wandered among the tables. "I didn't know we had so *many* delightful things in Pixie Hollow."

Tinker Bell's table gleamed with kettles, pans, and utensils. She held up a long-handled skillet. "Have you ever seen anything more beautiful than the shape of that handle?" she said in a hushed tone.

Rani smiled and moved on. The fairy circle buzzed with activity as the fairies proudly displayed their treasures. Some had used balloon carriers to bring their offerings through the rain. But some treasures were small and easy to carry. The cooking-talent fairies didn't even need a whole table. Their most valuable things fit into a little sandalwood box. Their treasures were recipe cards.

It was a wondrous bazaar. The dyeing-talent fairies displayed pots of dye in colors Rani had never even seen before. There were colors so rare they

didn't even have a name. One of the dyeing-talent fairies showed her a small vial of vivid pink dye. It was nestled in a silk pouch in a golden box. "It's the only vial of Volcano Pink left in Never Land. This dye was made from the last sunset before the eruption on Torth Mountain."

Rani walked over to the mining-talent fairies' table. The only thing on display was an old pick. Orren, a mining-talent sparrow man, lifted it up. "She's a beauty, isn't she?"

Rani smiled. "Yes. But tell me about it. What makes it a treasure?"

"That's the pick that opened up the biggest vein of Never pewter ever found," he said proudly.

A group of art-talent fairies across

the aisle scoffed at him. Bess said, "You're being silly, Orren. A pick isn't a treasure. A pick is a tool. A treasure is something like a painting or a sculpture."

At the next table, Queen Clarion's helpers laid out the queen's favorite shoes, which were made from woven gold threads.

"Now who's being silly," one of them said. "A treasure is something rare. You art-talent fairies turn out a dozen paintings a week. So how can they be treasures? Now *this* is a treasure." She held up a delicate piece of hand-made paper.

"What is that?" Rani asked.

"It's an invitation to a ball written in the queen's own hand, using the royal pen. See? The ink is purple and it glitters."

Behind the queen's helper, the sewing-talent fairies laughed. "An invitation! You think an invitation is a treasure? You're quite wrong. A treasure is something that takes time to create. Something that's made with skill and patience and creativity. Look around you. Every single fairy is wearing a beautiful, one-of-a-kind dress made especially for her. Any one of our dresses is more of a treasure than a pick or a painting or a pot or a note."

At this, the light-talent fairies rolled their eyes. "You sewing talents are so conceited," said Luna.

"*We* are not conceited," a sewing-

talent fairy retorted. "If anyone is conceited, it's the light talents."

Fira, who was setting out a beautiful glowworm lantern, scowled. "How dare you say that?"

"It's true," a passing music-talent fairy agreed. "You light talents always think you're the most important part of any party. You're always talking about how you have to rest and worrying about whether or not you'll have enough energy to glow. As if nothing else is important—not the food, not the dancing, and certainly not the music!" The music-talent fairy angrily folded her prized trumpet flower under her arm and turned away.

Fira stamped her foot. "That's the meanest thing anybody has ever said. Maybe the light talents just don't need to come to any more parties."

"Maybe you don't," Dulcie said. "And maybe the music talents don't need to come either. Everybody knows the most important part of a party is the food. But to hear the sewing talents tell it, the only reason fairies go to parties is so they can dress up."

"Well, well, well," a sarcastic voice said. "What's all this quarreling about?" The fast-flying fairy Vidia touched down in the midst of the arguing fairies.

"Vidia!" Rani exclaimed. "Have you brought your treasures?"

Vidia rolled her eyes. "No, dearest."

Rani suspected that Vidia's treasure was her secret stash of stolen fairy dust. Not that Vidia would admit it.

Vidia cast a scornful look around the fairy circle. "Let's face it, darlings, fairy dust is the only treasure worth having. Everything here is just a bunch of rubbish."

There were a number of outraged

shrieks. Suddenly, the pent-up frustration from all the rainy days overflowed.

The sewing talents accused the laundry talents of deliberately washing their best dresses in hot water so that they shrank. The garden fairies complained that the animal-talent fairies didn't make one bit of effort to explain to the birds and squirrels why they shouldn't eat their berries. "From now on, don't ask us to coax the insects out of your gardens!" the furious animal talents replied.

That angered cricket-whistling-talent fairies. After all, they said, *they* were often the ones who helped coax insects out of the gardens, not the animal fairies.

Soon, every single fairy was angry. Every single fairy felt unappreciated. Every single talent group was ready to take their treasures and go . . . when a terrible creaking noise brought them all up short.

Tink yelled, "Look at the canopy!"

Rani looked up. "Oh, no!"

While the fairies were arguing, the rain had collected on top of the canopy, causing it to sag. Before anyone could make a move, the entire canopy collapsed. Gallons of water and yards of wet cloth fell down, drenching all the fairies, along with their treasures, big and small.

8

Rani looked at the dismal mess. Broken tables, torn cloth, shattered pots, ripped garments, soggy paper, and muddy jewels were scattered everywhere. Every fairy was as upset as could be.

It was the rain that was making everyone so cranky and angry. It was the rain that was making everyone sad and gloomy. It was the rain that was ruining the peace and harmony of Pixie Hollow.

Rani whistled for Brother Dove. The faithful bird soared down. She climbed on his back.

"We're going to leave for a bit," she said. "What Pixie Hollow needs is some sunshine and some time to dry out, dry off, and calm down."

Rani and Brother Dove took to the sky. They circled around the clouds. Rani used the language of water—dots, plops, plinks, and gurgles. She urged the clouds to move quickly.

Brother Dove carried Rani out of the clouds until she was in front of the flock. They flew low over Never Land, leading the rain clouds away from Pixie Hollow and toward the forest.

Rani looked down. She saw the leaves on the trees tremble as the raindrops fell. Some of the trees were a bit brown, she noticed. But after a splash of rain, they seemed to brighten and stand up straighter.

Rani smiled. It was nice to bring rain where it was wanted and needed.

Rani wondered if other parts of Never Land needed rain. She asked Brother Dove to fly higher so she could get a better view. To the south, she saw a yellow field that should have been green. "That way," she told Brother Dove.

They flew over the field. Rani and Brother Dove let the clouds hover for hours, giving the field below a nice, long drink.

After they watered the field, they flew over a pond that seemed to be drying out. Rani and Brother Dove flew closer. The waterline was dangerously low. In a short time, there wouldn't be enough water in the pond to keep the fish alive.

So Rani and Brother Dove perched on a nearby tree limb and settled in for a long afternoon. The clouds hovered over the pond, slowly filling it.

As the water in the pond rose, fish jumped. The limp grass along the banks sprang up. Frogs leaped into the water, and schools of tadpoles skittered this way and that just below the surface.

Rani wondered where Dab was. Dab wasn't a fairy, but she still had an

important role to play. Every pond, field, garden, and creature in Never Land depended on rain to stay alive. Herding and moving the rain clouds across Never Land was Dab's role. If she had been a fairy, it would have been her talent.

Even though Rani wasn't a cloud keeper, bringing rain where it was needed was a way of using her water talent. As Rani thought this, a wave of happiness warmed her from head to toe. It was a wonderful feeling.

"How could Dab abandon her talent?" Rani asked out loud. "Wherever she is, it seems like she would be miserable."

Brother Dove made a noise in his throat. He pulled his wings in tighter.

Rani felt a pang of guilt. Poor Brother Dove. He wasn't a creature of the water, but he had spent the last three days soaked. She reached out and ran her hand down his wet feathers to show her gratitude.

Brother Dove cooed. Rani felt another wave of happiness as she thought of something she could do for him.

Tonight they would go back to the caves. Rani could sleep in the open, so the clouds would see her and stay calm. Brother Dove could sleep inside the cave where he would be warm and dry. She knew he would worry at first, but she would tell him to sleep well.

As long as I am using my talent to

do something good, Rani thought, *I will be fine.*

That night, Rani lay on a ledge just outside one of the caves. She stared up into the dark, wet night. Her mind raced, trying every combination of Pixie Hollow treasures she could think of.

"*Hear me, Dab, wherever you are. In the name of Pixie Hollow's three treasures—a paper-thin porcelain tea set, Queen Clarion's handwritten invitation, and Orren's pick—I wish you back . . . I wish you back . . . I wish you back!*

"*Hear me, Dab, wherever you are. In the name of Pixie Hollow's three treasures—Dulcie's recipes, Bess's sea*

glass, and Vidia's fairy dust—I wish you back . . . I wish you back . . . I wish you back!

"Hear me, Dab, wherever you are. In the name of Pixie Hollow's three treasures—Lily's giant buttercups, Fira's glowworm lantern, and Tink's skillet—

*I wish you back. . . I wish you back. . .
I wish you back!"*

But nothing happened. Eventually,
Rani's eyelids grew heavy and she fell
sound asleep.

9

RANI AND BROTHER Dove traveled
around Never Land for four days.
Everywhere they went they brought
fields to life, restored health to ponds,
and made gardens bloom.

Rani always kept her eye out for
Dab. Once or twice, she could have
sworn she heard Dab's laughter. But if
Dab the trickster was near, she had

learned to move faster than Rani's eyes could see.

By the end of the fourth day, Rani and Brother Dove headed back to Pixie Hollow. Rani knew what she had to do, and she needed to tell the others.

As they approached Pixie Hollow, Rani could see that the fairy circle had been cleared of debris. Crisp, dry laundry hung from lines strung about the Home Tree. And the garden-talent fairies were tilling the moist soil to plant new seeds.

When they saw Rani coming with the clouds behind her, the fairies scrambled. The laundry-talent fairies plucked clothes off the lines as fast as they could. And the garden fairies

darted indoors, dragging their baskets of seeds behind them.

Rani and Brother Dove landed. The fairies came out of their rooms and work spaces to greet them. They carried petal umbrellas and wore slickers.

Prilla came running through the crowd with Tinker Bell close behind her. "You're back!" Prilla cried happily.

Tink pulled on her bangs. "You can't imagine how much we missed you," she said in a gruff voice. Rani knew it was the voice Tink used when she was about to cry but didn't want anybody to know.

The crowd parted, and Queen Clarion hurried forward. Her helpers tried to keep pace with her and hold an umbrella over her head. But the queen moved too fast. She didn't care about getting wet.

"Welcome. You have been missed," she told Rani.

"And I missed all of you," Rani said. "But as you can see, the clouds are still following me. I haven't figured out how to make them stop."

The entire population of Pixie Hollow groaned.

"But don't worry," Rani said quickly. "I'm not staying."

Everyone gasped.

"What do you mean? You *can't* leave," Prilla insisted. "You can't solve a problem by running away from it."

"I'm not running away," Rani protested. "But every part of Never

Land needs rain eventually. Somebody has to keep these clouds moving and make sure that the rain gets where it needs to be. I guess that somebody is me."

"But what will we do without you?" Tink asked.

"I'll come back from time to time. When you need rain," Rani said. "But when you don't need rain, I'll be away."

Queen Clarion dabbed at her eyes with a gold-edged leafkerchief. "I fear that we have failed you. We have looked for treasure everywhere. And either we cannot find it, or we cannot agree on what it is."

Rani shook her head. "Don't feel bad. And don't worry. I'll be with the rain. As long as I can use my talent, I'll be fine."

Rani looked out at all the sad faces. Already, the rain was beginning to wilt their hairdos and dampen their wings. It was time to pack her things and go.

Twenty minutes later, Rani came out of the Home Tree. She carried a few spare tunics and her special conch shell tucked into a satchel.

Fira came rushing up. "The light talents have something for you to take." She placed a stone in Rani's hands. "It's a glow stone. It stores light during the day and glows in the night. It will give you comfort in the dark."

Rani was touched. After all the
trouble she had caused, it was nice of
Fira to worry about her.

A conducting-talent fairy lifted her
hands, and all the music talents began to
sing. It was the most cheerful melody
Rani had ever heard. And it was so

tuneful, she knew she would remember every note. "We wrote that especially for you," the conducting fairy told her. "It's a song to sing when you're lonely." Rani was grateful. She knew the tune would come in handy.

Soon, every talent group was pressing something into her hands. A flint for starting a fire. A bit of extra fairy dust. A warm dress with a hood. Her favorite cookies.

Finally, Rani was ready to go. She was happy. She was content. And she felt brave and eager for adventure. But when she saw Prilla and Tink's faces, she thought her heart might break.

"Let's go, Brother Dove," she whispered. "Let's go quickly before we all start to cry." Rani didn't mind crying in front of the other fairies. She did it all the time. But she knew Tink hated for anyone to see her cry.

Brother Dove spread his wings. But before he and Rani could take off, Tink came running toward them. "Wait!" she shouted. "Wait!"

Brother Dove lowered his wings.

"I'm going with you," Tink said, panting. "To keep you company."

"But you can't stand being wet," Rani argued.

"I'll just have to get used to it. Besides, it's not forever. We'll be back in a few weeks because Pixie Hollow will need the rain."

"That's right," Prilla said. "And

when you leave the next time, *I'll* go with you."

"We'll take turns!" Fira cried. "So you'll never be without a friend while you're away."

Rani began to cry. She had never been so touched. Yes, having a talent was wonderful. But she realized now that without friendship, life would be very lonely.

Another wave of happiness warmed Rani from head to toe. "Okay, Tink," she said. "Get your gear and let's go. It will be fun."

At that moment, Beck came flying rapidly toward them. "Wait up! Wait! Mother Dove wants to see Rani before she leaves!"

10

"Now, TELL ME everything from start to finish," Mother Dove instructed. She settled herself on her blue egg and fixed Rani with a kindly eye.

Rani sat down on the edge of Mother Dove's nest. She told her the whole story. She ended with a sigh. "I'd fly backward if I could, but I can't. I can only fly forward. So that's what I'm going to do. I just hope you'll forgive me for causing so much trouble."

Mother Dove's feathers ruffled. "Rani, my dear, that's why I wanted you to come. So that I could tell you this myself. No matter what you've done, no matter where you are, I will love you."

Another wave of warm happiness washed through Rani from head to toe.

"I would tell most fairies setting out on an adventure to stay safe and stay dry." Mother Dove chuckled. "But to you, I will just say *stay safe and stay happy.*"

"I *am* happy," Rani said gaily. "Isn't that odd? This should be the saddest day of my life. But I don't feel a bit sorry. In fact, I've never been so happy."

Mother Dove moved her wings a bit. "Oh? Why do you think that is?"

Rani thought hard. "Well, I guess because it's impossible to be unhappy when you know you have talent, friendship, and love. What more could you want? What more could you need? As long as you have those three things you . . ." Rani broke off. Her mouth fell open. Her eyes widened.

Mother Dove said nothing, but her own eyes twinkled.

Rani drew in her breath with a gasp. "Oh, Mother Dove," she whispered. "That's it, isn't it?"

Mother Dove chuckled.

"I've done it, haven't I? I've guessed the three treasures."

"There is only one way to find out," Mother Dove said.

Rani lifted her face and called out as loudly as she could: *"Hear me, Dab, wherever you are. In the name of Pixie Hollow's three treasures—talent, friendship, and love—I wish you back . . . I wish you back . . . I wish you back!"*

A huge clap of thunder shook the nest. It was followed by the sound of water pouring over a waterfall. Dab's bubbling laughter filled the air. And in a flash, she appeared, as shimmering as ever.

"Well!" she exclaimed. "I was beginning to give up on you. I can't believe you took so long to figure it out. Maybe fairies aren't as smart as I thought."

Rani laughed so hard that tears rolled down her cheeks. "I was looking for *things*," she said.

Dab snorted. "*Things!* Who cares about things? Everybody has *things*. Those aren't the treasures everyone envies and wishes they possessed. Everyone knows that the fairies are happy. And they are happy because they have talent, friendship, and love. So cherish your treasures, my friend. And don't make any more bargains with water sprites," she cautioned.

Dab wicked from nest to bush, then from ground to sky. Rani heard her talking to her clouds in the magic language of water—full of dots, plops, plinks, and gurgles.

Dab was gathering her clouds, calling them, herding them. Rani watched her work, admiring her bright quickness. Soon, the gray clouds were on the move.

Rani waved. But she didn't know if Dab waved back or not, because for the first time in days, the sun was shining in her eyes.

This is the end of
RANI AND THE THREE TREASURES.

Turn the page to read
RANI IN THE MERMAID LAGOON.

Rani
in the
Mermaid
Lagoon

Rani
in the
Mermaid
Lagoon

WRITTEN BY
LISA PAPADEMETRIOU

ILLUSTRATED BY
THE DISNEY STORYBOOK ARTISTS

RANDOM HOUSE 🏠 NEW YORK

1

RANI PAUSED AT the gleaming metal door
to Tinker Bell's workshop. She bit her lip.
I'm not going to cry, she told herself. *This
time, I'm not.* Rani could hear her friend
hammering away inside the teapot. Tink
was busy, as usual.

Tink was a pots-and-pans-talent fairy,
and the best fixer in Pixie Hollow. She
could fix almost anything—a ladle that

leaked, a stubborn pot that never boiled, a colander that refused to let water run through its holes. Rani was hoping that Tink could fix her problem.

Rani took a deep breath and walked into her friend's workshop. "Hi, Tink," she said.

With an impatient frown, Tinker Bell looked up from the copper pot she had been hammering. But when she saw Rani, she smiled, showing her dimples. "Rani!" she said. She put down her hammer. "What are you doing here? Why aren't you—"

"—making the fountain?" Rani finished. She did that sometimes—got excited and finished other fairies' sentences for them. "It's because—" Rani stopped.

"Because—" She tried again, but she didn't get any further before she burst into tears.

"Rani, what's wrong?" Tink flew over to her friend and patted her gently on the back. Her fingers avoided the place where Rani's wings used to be. Rani was a wingless fairy—the only one in Pixie Hollow. She had cut off her wings to save Never Land. That made her a hero. It also made her the only fairy who couldn't fly on her own. A bird named Brother Dove helped her when she needed him.

On the other hand, Rani was the only fairy in Pixie Hollow who could swim. Fairy wings become very, very heavy when they are wet. That's why fairies never swim—they'd get dragged under the water. And as a water-talent fairy, Rani *adored* water.

Rani pulled out a damp leafkerchief and blew her nose. Another crystal tear trickled down her face. "Tonight is the Fairy Dance," she began.

Tink grabbed a handful of fresh leafkerchiefs. She always kept some handy in case water-talent fairies came to visit. "I can't wait," she said.

The Fairy Dance was the reason she had been working so hard to fix the copper pot. The cooking-talent fairies needed it right away. The pot had recently decided it was a skillet, and served up stack after stack of pancakes, no matter what the cook was trying to make. But the cooking-talent fairies couldn't serve pancakes at the most important party of the month! Frowning, Tink tapped the pot with her tinker's hammer, but the dent in its side stubbornly refused to budge.

The Fairy Dance was held every full moon. That was when the moon was at its fattest, brightest, and merriest. All the talents worked together to make the party the best it could be. The light-talent fairies hung glowworms from the branches of the

Home Tree. They also set fireflies loose over the clearing where the dance was held. The baking-talent fairies made stacks of sweet, crisp butter cookies. The cooking-talent fairies made crustless mushroom sandwiches as light as a feather, and acorn caps full of pumpkin soup. The decoration-talent fairies made sure the leaves of the maple trees in Pixie Hollow sparkled. And the water-talent fairies made a fountain at the center of the clearing. The fountain was important because all the fairies danced around it.

Just thinking about the fountain made Rani burst into tears again. She wiped them away impatiently and took a deep breath. "You know I always make the large water jet that goes at the very top of the Fairy

Dance fountain," she started to explain.

"Of course you do," Tink said. "You make the prettiest jet in all of Pixie Hollow."

"Well, the other water-talent fairies think Humidia should do it." Tears filled Rani's eyes once more. Her nose began to run. "Because I can't fly. They said Brother Dove's flapping wings would mess up the shape of the jet when I placed it at the top of the fountain. They said his wings would probably destroy the whole fountain if we went too close!"

Tink tugged on her bangs. She knew how it felt to think you might be losing your talent. It felt *awful.* "The fountain won't be the same without your talent. That's—"

"—terrible," Rani finished, shaking her head. "I'm a water-talent fairy, and I can't even help with the water fountain!"

Rani squeezed her leafkerchief, dripping water onto the floor. She dabbed at her overflowing eyes again. Water-talent fairies are as full of liquid as a ripe, juicy berry. They perspire, cry, and sniffle more than other fairies. They just can't help it.

"Well," Tink said, "whether or not you work on the fountain, it's still a party. And you *love* parties. I'll save you a spot in the Fairy Dance. Until then, maybe you can use your talent to help another talent."

"Another talent?" Rani repeated. She pressed her lips together, thinking hard. "I can help the cooking-talent fairies boil the water," she said. She had done that once or twice before. It wasn't as much fun as working on the fountain, but it was better than nothing. In fact, maybe she could help the cooking-talent fairies make something delicious to eat. That would be fun, Rani realized. "Thanks, Tink. I'll go ask right now," she said as she hurried out the door.

"Don't mention it!" Tink called.

But Rani didn't hear her. She was on her way to the kitchen.

Rani stood at the edge of the fairy circle and sighed. She had already been to the huge kitchen in the Home Tree. She had asked if she could help the cooking-talent fairies boil water. But they had told Rani that the food was already prepared. Then

Rani had come to the clearing to see if she could help another talent. But everything was already done. There was nothing left for her to do.

A long table was heaped with all sorts of treats the cooking- and baking-talent fairies had whipped up. There were cream tarts, sticky muffins, and platters of mushroom sandwiches. The polishing-talent fairies had shined the forks, spoons, and knives until they gleamed. The table-setting-talent fairies were putting them out. The gardening-talent fairies had cleared the grounds and planted bright blue pansies around the edges. The light-talent fairies had already placed the glow-worms. The fireflies were gathering nearby.

"Moon and stars! The fountain looks beautiful, Rani," said a voice.

Rani turned and saw Fira smiling at her. Her eyes were twinkling. Fira, also known as Moth, was a light-talent fairy. She glowed more brightly than a normal Never fairy. Even the tips of her long, dark hair sparkled.

Fira looked back at the fountain. She paused thoughtfully. Fira often considered her words carefully before she spoke. "I just wish I could find a way to light it up," she said finally. "But whenever I try to get a flame near the water, it—"

"—goes out, I know," Rani agreed.

"Still, it looks very good," Fira said.

Rani sighed. "Thanks, but I didn't have anything to do with it. I can't fly, so Humidia took my job."

"Oh, Rani," Fira said.

Rani turned away. Tears prickled in her eyes . . . again.

"Try not to worry," Fira said. "You'll go to the dance tonight and have a wonderful time." She snapped, and a spark flew from her fingers. It swirled above their heads for a moment, then blinked out. "Dancing will help you forget all about the fountain."

Rani looked into Fira's smiling dark eyes, which shone with happy pinpoints of light. She knew Fira was trying to help. Rani gave her a watery smile.

Fira could see that her friend was still feeling sad. "Don't forget that you saved Mother Dove's egg," Fira pointed out. "You have more than one talent, Rani."

But there's only one talent I want, Rani

thought. Still, she knew there was no point in arguing. Humidia had made the fountain's jet. That was all there was to it. Now Rani had to try to enjoy the Fairy Dance as well as she could.

"Thanks, Fira," Rani said after a moment. "I'll see you tonight at the dance."

2

"Down there, Brother Dove!" Rani said excitedly. She leaned forward to peer over Brother Dove's neck as he swooped toward the fairy circle.

The fireflies winked. They—along with the glowworms—sent a soft light through the clearing. The fairy fountain sparkled at the center. It was tall, rising almost as high as the trunk of the sycamore that stood nearby. The music-talent fairies were already tuning their grass-reed instruments. Rani bit her lip. She was a little late.

Brother Dove started toward a spot just under the trees where several branches met. Stars twinkled in the gaps between the leaves. Fairies flitted about, forming three circles and practicing their cartwheels for the dance. Even nasty Vidia smiled as she watched from a short distance away.

"There she is!" Rani cried. She had spotted Tink hovering between Beck, an animal-talent fairy, and Terence, a dust-talent sparrow man.

Just then, the music-talent fairies struck up the first notes of the Fairy Dance melody.

"Hurry!" Rani cried. "The dance is

starting!" She wanted to take her usual place near Tink in the outer circle.

There were three circles in the Fairy Dance. All three circled in midair around the fairy fountain. The inner circle was the smallest and the easiest to dance in. The youngest fairies danced in this circle until they learned the dance. Then there was a middle circle. That was for fairies who knew the dance but weren't experts. The outer circle was the largest. It was also the hardest to dance in. There was a lot of twirling, flipping, and cartwheeling.

Sometimes, the outer-circle dancers changed direction and danced in the opposite way from the fairies in the middle circle. It was like what Clumsies called a square dance, only it was round. It was also much more difficult. All three circles were in constant motion, moving one way and then another and switching dancers.

Rani loved dancing in the outer circle. A fairy had to dance very quickly to keep up with the music. If she didn't keep up, she lost her place in the circle. Then she had to wait until the next song to dance again. This time, however, it would be different for Rani— she'd be on Brother Dove's back.

Brother Dove flew toward the outer circle of fairies. Luckily, there was no breeze that night. A gust of wind could make the dancers bump into each other.

"Rani! Over here!" Tink called. She and Beck flipped from the outer circle to the center circle, then out again. Terence was right beside Tink. *He's going to crash into someone if he isn't careful,* Rani thought. *He's paying more attention to Tink than to the other dancers around him!*

With two quick flaps of his wings, Brother Dove shot toward where Tink was doing a midair flip. But the musicians had reached the fastest part of the song. The fairies' wings were moving so fast they were humming.

"Fly me here!" the fairies sang as everyone turned a cartwheel to the left. *Clap-clap-clap!* "Fly me there!" Cartwheel to the right, and *clap-clap-clap!*

Rani knew she should be grateful to Brother Dove even to be a part of the Fairy Dance. But she couldn't help feeling left out as the other fairies flipped and zipped from one circle to the next. Since Brother

Dove was so much bigger than the fairies, he kept to the outer circle. Still, it was nice to join in the dance. . . .

"Whoa!" Rani cried. She stopped clapping to hold tightly to the soft, downy feathers at Brother Dove's neck as he did a little flip of his own. "Over there!" Rani pointed to the far side of the outer circle. Tink had flipped out of the inner circle and was now on the other side.

Rani stood up as Brother Dove flapped toward Tink. This was her favorite part of the dance. Kick and kick, then jump, jump, jump! A light little leap, then twirl to your right. . . .

My feet haven't forgotten, Rani thought. She started to move in time to the music. *I may not have wings, but I can still dance!* Rani grinned and twirled to her right—

Oh, no!

With a cry, Rani felt her foot slip from Brother Dove's back. She flailed her arms. A moment later, she plunged into empty space.

"Rani!" Tinker Bell shouted. She dove after her friend.

"Tink!" Terence cried. Around him, the dance turned into a jumble. Fairies crashed into each other.

The green grass of the clearing rushed up to meet Rani as she fell toward the ground. She didn't even have time to scream before she felt a yank on her arm. Her fall slowed slightly.

"Thanks, Tink!" Rani said with a gasp. But Tink wasn't strong enough to stop her. Now they were both falling.

There was another dreadful yank as

Terence caught Tink under the arms and struggled to hold her up.

Screams and gasps came from the fairies. Terence, Tink, and Rani crashed through the fountain, shattering it. Water showered everywhere. But they were moving more slowly now. Seconds later, Fira caught Rani's other arm. The strength of all

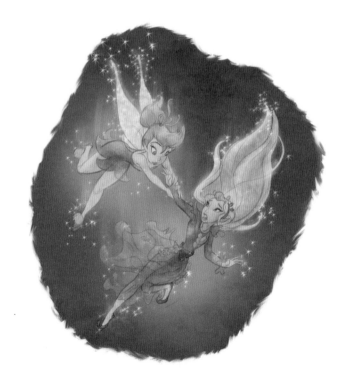

three fairies was enough. They set Rani down gently on the soft green grass.

For a moment, everything was silent. Rani looked around at the wreck she had caused. There was a floating knot of fairies whose wings had gotten tangled up. A sparrow man had plunged facefirst into a pot of pumpkin soup. One of Terence's wings was bent, and half of Tink's hair had come loose from her ponytail. All that was left of the fountain was a damp puddle on the grass. Rani's brand-new violet-petal dress was torn.

The musicians were quiet. The only sound Rani could hear was the beat of Brother Dove's wings as he landed beside her.

Tink's large blue eyes looked worried. "Rani, are you okay?"

Rani felt the hot tears begin to flow down her face. She whispered, "I didn't mean to—"

"Didn't mean to?" a voice interrupted. Cruel Vidia—the fastest of the fast-flying-talent fairies—flew down to land beside Rani. Tinker Bell folded her arms across her chest and glared at Vidia.

"Darling, you must understand that we're all simply *worried* about you," Vidia went on with a touch too much sugar in her voice. Her red lips curled into a smile. "Why, a fairy with no wings couldn't *hope* to be a part of the Fairy Dance," Vidia said. "I'm surprised you even tried."

"Be quiet, Vidia," Fira snapped. "She was doing fine until—"

"Until she ruined the entire thing,

including her own talent's fountain?" Vidia finished. "Sweetie, it isn't your fault that you wrecked the dance," she said to Rani. "We all understand that you were only trying to belong. But you have to accept the fact that without your wings, you're useless."

"Vidia—" Tink growled. She balled her tiny fists in rage.

But Rani didn't hear the end of Tink's sentence. She had already started running. She didn't stop even when she heard Tinker Bell calling her name.

Rani sat beneath a tall willow tree, weeping. She cried until there was a puddle all around her. She cried until she had no more tears left. This had never happened to Rani before. She'd always been full of water.

When her sobs ended, the dark woods were silent. Rani was in a part of the forest she didn't know. "I should go back to the

Home Tree," she said aloud. Her voice skipped between the trees and disappeared into the blackness of the night. Rani took a step toward the Home Tree. She could picture its comforting branches, the brightly lit rooms full of fairies.

Rani sighed. "They don't want me," she said, feeling sorry for herself. But where else could she go? "Well," she reasoned, "I can't go back. So I might as well go forward." And with that, she turned and walked farther into the woods.

Past the tall, dark trees and beyond a moonlit clearing, Rani came to a little trickling branch of Havendish Stream. She picked up a small pebble and dropped it into the water. Then she walked to the edge of the stream and stepped in up to her ankles.

The cool, clear water ran over her tired feet. She felt her mood lift. With a kick, Rani splashed a frog that was sitting by the side of the stream. She laughed as he croaked and flopped into the water.

Rani splashed around a little longer, then made her way back to shore. She was just about to step out of the stream when she saw it—a pretty little birch-bark canoe. Water-talent fairies sometimes used them to go exploring. This one looked as if it had been swept downstream when a careless fairy didn't tie it up properly.

"It's almost as though someone left it here for me," Rani said to herself.

A paddle lay in a puddle of water in the bottom of the canoe. Rani moved her hand over the puddle. In a moment, the water formed a ball. Rani picked it up and tossed it into the river, where it dissolved into the rest of the water. She ran her hands over the whole boat, making sure it was watertight. Then she stepped into the canoe.

Moonlight sparkled on the water as Rani paddled downstream. A small waterfall whispered gently. Rani didn't know

where she was going. As long as it was away from the other fairies, it was fine with her.

Peeking over the edge of the canoe, Rani looked down at her small, heart-shaped face reflected in the water. *From the front, I still look like a normal fairy,* she thought. She reached out and touched the water. Her face dissolved into ripples.

Rani cupped water in her hand and brought it to her lips. "Good-bye, Tinker Bell," she whispered into the water. "I'll miss you. You are my forever friend, but I can't stay with the fairies anymore."

She blew on the water, and it grew and stretched until it was a large bubble. Rani lifted her hand into the air. The bubble shimmered in front of her for a moment before it floated away. A breeze pushed it toward the Home Tree, where it would find Tink. Rani had sent many of these bubble messages before. They never failed.

With a sigh, Rani leaned back. She watched the stars overhead as the canoe carried her downstream. She saw a long, moss-covered log lying across the stream, like a bridge. Just as Rani's canoe passed under the log, she heard a soft splash.

What was that? Rani wondered. She sat up in the canoe. Looking over the side, she saw a whiplike motion in the dark water behind her. It was a water snake!

Rani's heart fluttered in her chest. Snakes were almost as dangerous to fairies as hawks were. She dipped her paddle in the water, straining with all her might. The canoe started to pull away. A glance backward told her that the snake was moving quickly.

"Hurry, hurry!" Rani urged herself. The canoe sped forward. Suddenly, Rani heard a soft hissing sound.

She turned, expecting the snake to be right on top of her. But he was still several canoe lengths away.

Startled, Rani faced forward. The hissing she heard wasn't the snake. It was the hiss water makes as it races over rocks. "Oh, no!" Rani cried. She dug her paddle into the water, trying to slow the canoe.

Hiss!

Behind her, the water snake drew level with the canoe. He was going to strike! "Get back!" Rani shouted. She stood and raised her paddle.

In a flash, the snake lunged forward. Rani brought her paddle down on his head. The snake bent under the force of the blow, then pulled back. His forked tongue flickered in and out. His black eyes narrowed in fury.

Rani thought fast. When the snake struck, she held back for an extra moment. Just as the snake's fangs were about to close over her, she shoved her paddle between his jaws.

The snake thrashed from side to side. Water splashed wildly, but the paddle didn't budge. He couldn't close his mouth!

Rani started to relax. But then she remembered that she had another problem. The hiss had become a roar.

Turning toward the front of the canoe,

Rani saw the white water just ahead. She grabbed the side of the boat. It swayed and rocked. Rani let out a scream. Her ears were filled with the noise of the rapids. Her stomach felt sick from the motion.

I can't hang on! Rani thought. Her hand slipped from the side of the canoe.

The canoe hit the largest rock in the rapids. The boat ripped apart with the force of the blow. Rani was tossed into the water.

She struggled against the current, but it was too strong. Finally, she gave up and let the water swallow her.

4

"I KNOW WHAT this is. . . . I've seen one before. It's a fairy."

"It can't be a fairy. It doesn't have a wand. Or wings."

"Not all fairies have wands, you know."

"Yes, they do."

"Shhh! It's moving."

Rani coughed. Her eyes fluttered open. At first, all she could see was a bright light and a shadow. Finally, the world came into focus. Someone was looking down at her curiously. She had beautiful green eyes, a delicate nose, yellow-green hair—and skin made of tiny scales.

A mermaid! Rani thought. A second mermaid with blue eyes and blue-green hair was beside the first one.

Rani sat up, then wished she hadn't moved so quickly. Her whole body was sore. As she looked around, she saw that she was lying on the shore. The mermaids leaned over her with their tails still in the water.

"Where am I?" Rani asked.

"She wants to know where she is," the blue-eyed mermaid said.

"I heard her," the green-eyed one snapped. She looked down at Rani. "You're

where Havendish Stream meets the Mermaid Lagoon," she told Rani.

"Are you a fairy?" the other one asked.

Rani coughed again. "Yes."

"There," the green-eyed mermaid said in a haughty way. "Didn't I tell you? They don't *all* have wands."

Rani looked at the green-eyed mermaid carefully. "I think I know you," she said. "Aren't you . . . Soop?"

The mermaid smiled. Soop's name wasn't really Soop, but only other mermaids could pronounce her real name. "I'm not Soop," she said. "Though creatures who don't know better think we look alike. I'm Oola. And who are you?"

"I'm Rani."

"If you're a fairy," the other mermaid said, "where are your wings?"

"Oh, be quiet, Mara," Oola grumbled. (Mara wasn't the other mermaid's name either, but it was the only part Rani could catch.) "Isn't it obvious? She cut them off so that she could swim with mermaids."

Mara's eyes widened. "You did?"

"Well . . ." Rani had cut off her wings because she'd needed to ask the mermaids for one of their beautiful combs to save Mother Dove's egg. So in a way, she *had* cut off her wings to swim with mermaids. ". . . yes. I guess so."

Mara gasped in admiration. She looked Rani over from head to toe. Rani blushed. She knew she was a mess. Her blond hair was tangled, and her violet dress—already torn from her fall at the Fairy Dance—was now practically in rags. "So," Mara said, "what are you doing—"

"—here?" Rani shook her head. "I'm running away."

The mermaids gasped. "Running away!" Oola repeated.

"I would never leave the Mermaid Lagoon," Mara said.

"Mara!" Oola snapped. "Don't insult the fairy. Not everyone lives in a place as nice as the Mermaid Lagoon."

"Oh, Pixie Hollow is beautiful," Rani put in quickly.

Oola smiled. But she didn't look as though she believed Rani. "Of course it is."

Rani couldn't think of anything to say after that.

Oola flicked her yellow-green tail thoughtfully as Rani toyed with a handful of water. Cupping it in her palms, Rani turned the drop into a ball, then stretched it so that it had a forked tongue and a long tail. She breathed on it, and the water snake's tail flickered.

"How did you do that?" Oola asked.

Rani shrugged. "I'm a water-talent fairy," she explained. "Water is my joy."

Reaching out a finger, Oola touched the water snake. It melted right away, falling back into the stream with a tiny splash. Oola laughed. "I guess I don't have any water talent," she said.

"Mermaids have different talents," Rani said, thinking about how graceful and lovely Oola and Mara were.

"Where will you go now?" Mara asked.

Rani sighed. "I don't know," she admitted.

Leaning over, Oola whispered something in Mara's ear. Mara's blue eyes widened, and she whispered something back to Oola. Oola nodded.

"We think you should come and live with us," Oola told Rani.

"You'd like it," Mara agreed.

"Me?" Rani flushed with pride. These beautiful mermaids wanted her to live with them? Underwater? The fairy's heart fluttered with excitement.

"You seem very happy in water," Oola pointed out.

Rani's smile faded. "But I can't breathe underwater," she said. To *live* underwater she would need a lot of air. Then Rani remembered the bubble message she had made for Tink. Couldn't she make a few bubbles like that and wear them as a necklace? Anytime she wanted to breathe, she could just pop one in her mouth—

"And take a breath!" Rani said aloud. She was so excited that she stood straight up.

Oola held out her hand, and Rani stepped onto it. "You'll be like a tiny mermaid," Oola said. She kindly ignored the fact that Rani didn't have scales . . . or a tail.

Rani smiled. She was off on an underwater adventure!

5

RANI LOOKED AROUND in amazement as they made their way through the mermaid lagoon.

A cloud of brilliant silver-blue fish darted past, and Rani saw three mermaids sitting on a rock. A merman inspected a field of bright green seaweed—he was the palace chef and was gathering salad greens. Two small merboys chased each other through a patch of coral.

"How much farther to the castle?" Rani asked Oola. They had already been swimming for quite a while. Rani was thankful that she had thought of the bubble necklace. It was easy to breathe that way. Every time she put a bubble in her mouth, it was like taking a gulp of air. And if all else failed, she could always use the wind room.

The wind room was a room full of air that the mermaids used when their gills got tired. Unfortunately, the room reeked of fish. And Rani couldn't take the room with her if she wanted to leave the mermaid palace. All in all, the bubble necklace made it much easier to stay underwater.

"It isn't far," Oola replied. "You'll be able to see it once we swim over this hill."

Rani gasped when she caught sight of

the castle. The mermaids' palace was made of mother-of-pearl. It gleamed in the sparkling underwater light. To Rani, it seemed huge. It reached from the floor of the lagoon halfway to the surface.

Rani had always thought that the Home Tree was the most beautiful place on earth, but now she wasn't so sure.

"And you all live there?" Rani asked.

"Every mermaid and merman has a room in the palace," Oola told her.

Now, you might be wondering how it was that Rani and Oola were talking underwater. It was really quite easy if you had a mermaid to show you how to do it. The trick wasn't in the talking . . . it was in the *listening*. Rani had to listen very carefully to each bubble that came out of Oola's mouth. It took a bit of practice, but once

Rani knew how, it was as simple as talking with the fairies in Pixie Hollow.

Oola and Mara swam through the castle. From her seat in Oola's hand, Rani admired everything. In every room, there were bunches of flowering seaweed arranged in tall pink spiral shells. In one room, two large hermit crabs chased each other playfully around a bed made from a giant clamshell.

Throughout the castle, conch shells hid lights that gave off a golden glow. Rani wondered what the lights were made of. They were very pretty.

"Let's go to the dressing room," Mara suggested. "The others will probably be there."

"Oh, let's not," Oola snapped. She was beginning to think of Rani as *her* fairy, and she didn't want to share her with the others. But Voona—a mermaid with a wild mane of yellow-orange hair—caught sight of them.

"Oooh, what do you have there?" Voona asked. She swam right up to Oola and stared at Rani. Her golden eyes widened. "Oh, my goodness—wherever did you get it? It's so strange!"

"I'm Rani," said Rani.

Voona shrieked. "It talks!"

"She's a fairy," Oola explained.

"She is? Where is her wand?" Voona demanded. "Oh, my goodness, we have to show the others right away!" She half pulled, half shoved Oola through a nearby door. "Girls! Girls! Look what we found!"

Soon, a cluster of chattering mermaids surrounded Rani.

"Oh, my gosh! What *is* it?"

"Is it *alive?*"

"How peculiar!"

"It's a fairy," Mara said proudly.

"It *is?*" The mermaids gaped at Rani, who blushed.

"Oh, look—it's turning red," Voona said.

Rani wished the mermaids wouldn't talk about her as though she weren't there. *But how do I ask them to stop without being rude?* she wondered.

Finally, Oola stepped in. "She's a fairy, and she's come to live with us . . . me. See? She cut off her wings to swim with the mermaids." Oola pointed to the place where Rani's wings used to be.

The mermaids gasped.

"And," Mara added, "she's had an adventure!"

"No wonder she looks such a mess," Voona said.

Rani blushed even harder, remembering her torn dress. She knew she wasn't looking her best.

"We can dress her up!" one of the mermaids cried.

"Oh, yes! Oh, yes!" the other mermaids agreed. There was a general bustle as they swam to different corners of the room. Each one collected something to help.

Rani sat at the center of a tall table. Mara began to brush her hair. Meanwhile, Oola pulled out a turquoise sea-silk handkerchief and started to make a new dress for Rani. A mermaid with violet hair painted Rani's lips with coral lip gloss.

Another mermaid found a tiny bone pin with a sparkly red jewel at the top. The mermaid took a pin that was similar—only much, much larger—and tied up her own hair with it. Then she told Rani to do the same. Rani did the best she could, but she was sure her hair didn't look as pretty as the mermaid's.

"Oh, much better!" Voona clapped her hands. "This fairy is absolutely adorable—I have to get one!"

Rani smiled as she looked down at the

sea-silk dress. It was the most beautiful thing she had ever worn. "Thank you," she said to her new friends.

"That was fun," Oola said.

Rani touched the red jewel in her hair. She had never had anything so fancy before. "Is there going to be a party?" she asked.

The mermaids stared at her.

"A par-tee?" Voona repeated.

"What's that?" Oola asked.

"A party," Rani said. "You know, where you and your friends dance and play music and eat and have a good time?"

"Sounds like fun!" Mara chirped.

"Oh, it is fun!" Rani said eagerly. "It's very fun!"

"I could wear my new shell necklace!" Mara cried.

"And I could wear my pearl comb,"
said another mermaid. Immediately, all the
mermaids began to plan what to wear.

"Oh!" Oola suddenly wailed. "Oh—it's
too terrible!"

"What is it, Oola?" Mara asked. The
other mermaids fell quiet.

"I couldn't possibly think of going to a
par-tee without my golden ring!" Oola wailed.

The mermaids were silent.

"Where is it?" Rani asked.

"I dropped it," Oola said, "down
Starfish Gap."

The other mermaids murmured and
shook their heads.

"It's a very deep, narrow gap," Oola
explained. "I'll never get it back." She
sighed loudly. She looked at Rani. Then
she sighed again.

Rani looked around at the roomful of sad mermaids. It seemed as if the party would never happen now. "Well . . . ," she said slowly, ". . . maybe I could go get it."

"Yes!" Mara cried. "Yes, Rani is small enough to fit in the gap!"

"Oh, would you?" Oola exclaimed. "That would be wonderful!"

The mermaids need me, Rani thought with a smile. *They need my help to get the ring. They don't even know how to have a party. I'll have to show them what to do!* "And then we can have our party?" she asked.

"Yes, of course!" Oola promised.

"Well, then," Rani said bravely, "just show me where it is."

6

"Are you sure it's in there?" Rani asked. She studied the deep, narrow crack in the ocean floor. It was so dark, she couldn't see more than two feet down.

"Oh, yes," Oola assured her. "I dropped it here last week."

"I saw it fall in," Mara added. "It was right by this yellow rock."

Rani hesitated. "It's very dark down there."

"Oh, don't worry about that," Voona said. "We'll hold up this light for you." She held out a conch shell filled with glowing pink seaweed.

Rani stepped forward uncertainly. The light did help, at least a little. She could see that Starfish Gap was lined with plants and corals. It didn't look as though there was anything dangerous down there. Still, it was a strange place, and Rani couldn't see all the way to the bottom. "Are you sure you need this ring?" she asked.

"I couldn't think of going to a par-tee without it," Oola said.

Rani sighed. It was clear she was going to have to get the ring. She plucked a particularly large bubble from her necklace and popped it into her mouth, taking a

deep breath. Then she dove over the edge of Starfish Gap.

The mermaids had told the truth. The gap was too narrow for anyone but a fairy. When she reached out her arms, Rani could touch both sides with her fingertips. The walls were rough.

Rani kicked harder, swimming down, down, down. Darkness began to close over her, and she stopped to look up. There, at the top, a long, long way up, were five beautiful mermaid faces. Oola held the light higher, and it cast its strange glow deeper into the gap and made eerie shadows on the walls.

"You're almost there!" Oola called. Her yellow-green hair floated around her face.

Rani looked down. She didn't feel as though she was almost there. She couldn't see the bottom and had no idea how far away it was. She wished she had thought to ask the mermaids how long she would have to swim to reach the floor of the gap.

But Rani wasn't afraid. She knew that the mermaids were waiting for her at the top. And she thought about how much fun they would have at the party.

It can be just like the Fairy Dance, Rani thought happily. *I'm sure the mermaids can do flips in the water as easily as we can in the air. I'll teach them the steps to the Fairy Dance. And I can do it with them! It will be just like flying. In fact, it will be better!*

Suddenly, a large rock loomed up before Rani. She squinted. There it was—

the bottom of Starfish Gap! Sure enough, in the pale light cast by the seaweed lantern, Rani saw a small circle of gold set with a purple stone. She swam toward it.

But just as she reached for it, the light overhead went out.

Rani paused, holding still. *What happened?* she wondered. "Oola?" she called.

There was no answer.

Rani's heart thudded in her chest. She looked up. All she could see was deep black velvety darkness. "Voona?" she shouted. "Mara! Where are you?"

She waited, listening hard. Rani thought she heard the far-off sound of a giggle, but none of the mermaids shouted down to her.

Don't be afraid, Rani told herself. *There's nothing down here.*

Rani bit her lip. She knew she was alone. Still, the hairs on the back of her neck were standing on end, as though someone were watching her. A picture of the water snake flashed through her mind.

"There are no water snakes in Starfish Gap," Rani said aloud. Her voice sounded strange and echoey. How could she be sure there were no water snakes down there? And what if there was something worse? Like a giant crab? Or a fish with huge teeth?

"Oh, stop it," Rani scolded herself. "You're here to find the ring. Just get it and swim back to the top."

Swallowing hard, Rani reached out her hands. In a moment, her fingers touched the smooth, round ring. She hooked it over her shoulder and began to swim toward the top of the gap.

The seconds seemed to crawl by as Rani swam through the darkness. She couldn't tell how far she had come or how much farther it was to the top. Rani traced her fingers over her bubble necklace nervously. She reminded herself that she had plenty of air.

After what seemed like forever, Rani noticed that the walls around her had turned a dark, shadowy gray. A little higher, she saw a cluster of seaweed that looked like a bunch of trumpets. With another kick, Rani found herself at the top of the gap.

"I'm back!" Rani called. "I found it!"

But the mermaids weren't there.

RANI SWAM OVER to the yellow rock. The seaweed lantern was overturned beside it. Brilliant pink seaweed lay scattered where it had spilled from the shell.

"Oola?" Rani called. "Mara? I found the ring!"

There was no answer.

Rani's heart thumped wildly in her chest. She knew that the Mermaid Lagoon held many dangers. There were lightning eels, which gave off an electric shock whenever something touched them. There were the small but fierce saberfish, which had teeth that were longer than their fins. There were tusked Never sharks. These sharks usually left others alone. But when they were angry, they could be ferocious. And, Rani thought, there were probably other dangers, too. Ones she hadn't heard about.

Rani felt certain that the mermaids needed her help. *They wouldn't have left me alone unless something happened,* she thought.

Just then, Rani heard a faint splashing noise coming from somewhere above her. Without thinking, she began to swim toward the sound.

Rani swam as hard as she could. She kicked her legs and strained her arms. *If only I were a mermaid,* she thought, *I could swim so much faster!* A bed of clams snapped shut as she swam past. A small school of scissorfish chased each other through a red and orange coral forest. But the mermaids were nowhere to be found.

Finally, Rani stopped and looked around. She wasn't sure which way to go.

Suddenly, there was a splash overhead. Then another splash, and a shriek. Rani looked up. Something large and silver was heading toward her. With a quick kick, she swam to the side. The silver thing dropped past her.

Then a flash of yellow-green darted by, like a ribbon in a fast breeze. It took a moment for Rani to realize that the yellow-green flash was Oola. She was chasing the silver thing.

Below her, Oola stopped. "I got it!" she shouted happily.

"Oola?" Rani called.

Looking up, the mermaid noticed Rani for the first time. "Oh, Rani, there you are!" she said in a rush. Oola swam over to the fairy and held out a large, heavy-looking silver mirror. "Look at what Peter Pan brought us," Oola said. "He stole it from the pirates—isn't that exciting?" She held it up and looked at herself.

Rani frowned. "I was worried that something had happened to you," she said.

Oola's yellow eyebrows drew together in confusion. "But why, silly fairy?" she asked. "What could happen?"

"Well . . . ," Rani began. Didn't Oola remember that she had gone down into the dark gap to get her ring? "I was down in

Starfish Gap, and the light went out, and—"

Just then Voona called Oola's name.

Voona's head broke down through the surface of the water. Her wild orange and yellow hair floated around her face.

"There you are." Voona swam over, a pout on her full lips. "It's just like you to hog Peter's present all for yourself."

There was a splash, followed by two more. Mara swam over with two mermaids right behind her. "What do you think you're doing, Oola?" Mara demanded. "Give us the mirror!" She reached for it, but Oola held it out of reach.

"I was just talking to my fairy," Oola huffed.

My fairy? Rani thought with a frown. But all the mermaids had turned to look at her. Clearing her throat, Rani pulled the ring off her shoulder and held it out in both hands. "I found the ring," she said.

"Oh! My ring!" Oola dropped the mirror and looked at the golden ring with the glittering purple stone. She snatched it from Rani's hands and slipped it over her slender finger.

The other mermaids gathered around. They oohed and ahhed over the ring. Rani couldn't help noticing that they seemed to have forgotten all about the mirror. *Just like they forgot about me*, she realized.

"I love purple," Mara said, running her hand through her blue and green hair. A comb with purple pearls was tucked into her locks.

Rani smiled. "So now we can have the party?" she asked eagerly.

But the mermaids didn't seem to hear.

"Well, yes, I suppose purple is all right," Voona said. She wagged her tail. "But it doesn't look very good on Oola."

Oola gaped at Voona. "It doesn't?" she asked.

Voona sneered. "It clashes with your hair."

Mara gasped. "She's right!"

"Purple doesn't go at all with green and yellow hair," pointed out a mermaid wearing a coral necklace that went perfectly with her red hair.

"Oh, how horrible!" said a mermaid with pink hair.

Oola's face turned a deep shade of green (that was how she looked when she was blushing). Yanking off the ring, she tossed it as far as it would go. It floated away and then down, down. It finally landed on a purple rock, where it bounced off . . . and dropped back down into Starfish Gap.

Rani stared at the gap in shock. The mermaids had sent her all the way down there for the ring, and now Oola had just thrown it back!

"Where did the mirror go?" Voona asked.

"I'll get it!" Mara called, starting toward the bottom of the lagoon.

"Wait a minute," Rani said. "Wait."

Pausing, Mara looked up at Rani expectantly. "What is it?"

Rani didn't know what to say. The mermaids were not going to say they were sorry for sending her into the gap, or for leaving her there. Still, she wanted to think that she hadn't gone to all that trouble for nothing. "Well . . . uh . . . I was wondering . . . When were we going to have the party?"

"Oh, that." Oola shrugged. "Well, we could have it now, I suppose."

Mara rolled her eyes. "But I wanted to look at the mirror!"

"We can have the par-tee quickly," Voona suggested. "And then we can look in the mirror."

Rani shook her head. "No, no—you don't understand. We can't have a party right away. We have to get ready for it. You all have to learn the steps to the dance, and we have to make the food and plan the music. There's a lot of work to be done!"

All the mermaids were silent. Then, suddenly, they erupted into laughter. They hooted and guffawed, and chortled and giggled. Oola laughed until tears streamed out of her eyes, although, of course, no one could see that underwater.

"What's so funny?" Rani demanded.

"Hoo-hoo!" Voona said to the other mermaids. "The fairy wants to know what's—"

"—funny," Rani finished for her. "Yes, what's so funny?"

The mermaids laughed even harder. They chuckled. They howled. They snickered and snorted. Rani frowned. She liked the mermaids less and less by the minute.

"Mermaids don't work!" Oola finally said.

"But the work is half the fun," Rani protested.

Finally, the mermaids stopped laughing. They all looked at Rani as though she were crazy. Rani felt herself blush.

"I'll go get the mirror," Mara said, and she swam away.

"Would you like to look in the mirror?" Oola asked gently. Rani wondered whether the mermaid felt a little sorry for her.

"Don't be silly," Voona snapped.

"Why would Rani want to look in the mirror? She isn't half as pretty as a mermaid! Besides, she's too little to hold it. She'd probably break it."

A wave of embarrassment rolled over Rani. She wished she could climb into a clamshell and hide. She couldn't help it that she didn't look like a mermaid. She was a fairy! And of course she wasn't as big as the mermaids or as graceful as they were in water. How could she be?

For a moment, Rani hoped Oola would disagree, but she only said, "You're right, Voona."

Mara swam up with the mirror in her hand. "I've got it!" she cried. Then she swam away, and the other mermaids swam after her. Rani was alone.

8

Rani sat down on a rock to think. "It looks like I don't really fit in anywhere." She sighed. She watched a fat blue blowfish dart behind a large tree of coral. "But I do like it down here. It's very pretty."

Soft light filtered through the water. It reminded Rani of the sunbeams that sifted through the Home Tree's green leaves. Two chubby striped brown flitterfish swam around and around a rock. Rani giggled. The fish looked like the chipmunks that lived in Pixie Hollow. A slow brown turtle swam past, as purposeful as a beaver on its way to build a dam in Havendish Stream.

Rani swam along, noticing other things that were like those in Pixie Hollow. There were corals shaped like twigs, a flying fish that looked like a sparrow, and anemones that looked like bushes.

Rani swam over to the flitterfish.

The two fish paused, gaping at her with huge round eyes. They were perfectly still, unable to decide whether Rani was dangerous.

"Hello," Rani said.

The fish darted away. In a moment, Rani couldn't even see them anymore. A cloud of bubbles floated where the fish had been.

"I guess they're shy," Rani said aloud.

Next, Rani paddled over to the brown turtle. Rani wasn't an animal-talent fairy. Still, she knew that the Havendish beavers were very friendly. "Excuse me!" Rani called. She tried to catch up to the turtle.

The turtle glanced at Rani out of the corner of his eye. He didn't stop or even slow down.

Rani tried again. "Pardon me. May I swim with you?"

The turtle kicked his flippers. He darted far ahead of Rani. She couldn't catch up. "Gee," she said to herself, "the creatures around here sure are unfriendly."

Just then, Rani caught sight of a patch

of bright blue seaweed. It was shaking back and forth.

Is the seaweed caught in a water current? Rani wondered. *Or is this some strange underwater plant that can move by itself?*

Rani swam over to take a closer look. She stared at the seaweed, then reached out to touch it. The moment she did, a long snout popped out and batted her hand away.

Rani darted backward. The leaves of seaweed parted to show a golden pink sea horse thrashing about. His eyes were wild as he looked at Rani. He was still for a moment, then shook back and forth, rearing his head and whipping his tail.

Rani moved a little closer to the sea horse, and he thrashed again. He clearly

was afraid of her. *Why doesn't he swim away?*
Rani wondered.

"What's the matter, sea horse?" Rani
asked in the tone of voice she had heard
animal-talent fairies use when talking to
a skittish animal. "Let me see," she said
gently.

Rani felt a little nervous. If she had been in Pixie Hollow, she would have run for Beck or one of the other animal-talent fairies. *Then again*, Rani thought, *I am a water-talent fairy, and this sea horse is a water animal. Maybe I can help.*

Reaching out, she touched the rough surface of the sea horse's body. She expected him to buck, but he didn't. He was perfectly still. Rani looked at him more closely and saw that his tail was caught in a length of fishing line. The line was tangled in the seaweed, and the sea horse couldn't escape.

"Oh, you poor thing," Rani said. "You're all tangled up! Don't worry, I'll help you."

The sea horse eyed Rani nervously while she pulled at the stubborn knots with

her tiny fingers. Once, she yanked a little too hard. The sea horse bucked.

Rani patted him. "Quiet down now, and I'll help you," she told the sea horse in a low voice. "We're almost there." The sea horse settled down, and Rani went to work on the knots again.

Over, under, through the loop. A tiny knot here, leading to a bigger knot there, then three more tiny knots. Finally, there were only two strands left. Rani pulled the fishing line away, and the sea horse was free.

"I did it!" Rani cried. "I did it!"

But she didn't get to celebrate for very long. The moment he was free, the sea horse raced away. He didn't even look back in Rani's direction.

Rani burst into tears. She couldn't help it. After all that work, even the sea horse didn't like her!

9

RANI CRIED AND cried, and her nose began to run, and then she got the hiccups. This was very uncomfortable underwater, and it only made her cry harder. It seemed as though no matter how hard she tried, nobody had any use for her!

Just then, Rani felt a gentle nudge at her hand. When she looked up, she saw the sea horse. He was carrying something in his mouth.

"Oh, hello," Rani said uncertainly.

Ducking his head, the sea horse dropped the object at Rani's feet. It was a large golden pearl. He looked up and nudged it toward her with his long snout. Then he looked at her again.

"A present?" Rani asked. "For me?"

The sea horse swam around in an excited circle. He nudged the pearl again, so that it was a little closer to Rani's feet. Rani reached down and picked up the pearl. It was large—about the size of an acorn. When Rani held it up, she saw that it glowed softly with its own golden light. Rani knew instantly that this was no ordinary pearl. It was magical.

"It's beautiful," Rani whispered. She turned to the sea horse. "Thank you."

The sea horse butted his head against

her hand and turned so his back was facing her. He looked over his shoulder at Rani.

"Do you . . . do you want me to ride on your back?" Rani pointed to herself and pointed to the sea horse.

The sea horse turned another circle. He pulled up next to Rani. She took that to mean yes.

Rani giggled. "Well," she said, "I've ridden on the back of a dove. I guess I could ride a sea horse." Cradling the pearl in her left arm, Rani carefully climbed onto the sea horse's back. She leaned forward and wrapped her right arm around his neck. The moment he felt her holding on, the sea horse took off.

He swam quickly, headed for the deepest part of the lagoon. Rani clung tightly to his neck. She remembered flying with

Brother Dove and felt a pang. She missed Brother Dove. She missed feeling the wind on her face.

The truth was, she missed Pixie Hollow.

Soon they entered an underwater garden. A small school of bright blue fish swept through an orange anemone. A yellow fish with purple spots scooted over a cluster of green seaweed. Everywhere she looked, Rani saw a rainbow of brilliant colors—purples and blues, greens and reds, spots and stripes and patterns she had never seen before.

"It's lovely," Rani whispered.

The sea horse seemed to understand what she had said, because he turned in a happy circle and moved forward through the garden.

In a few minutes, they left the underwater garden behind. The sea horse swam quickly toward a large shape in the distance. At first, Rani wasn't sure what it was. It looked like a mountain.

When they were a little closer, Rani gasped. Now she could tell what the mountain was!

"A sunken ship!" Rani exclaimed. She stared at the huge Clumsy ship as she and the sea horse swam past. It was larger than she ever could have imagined—even larger than the mermaid palace!

The sea horse swam up to a wall of rock with a small opening at the bottom.

"A cave?" Rani asked.

In answer, the sea horse ducked into the opening, which led to a long tunnel. It was very dark, but Rani wasn't afraid the way she had been when she was at the bottom of Starfish Gap. After all, she wasn't alone now. And she was starting to understand that the sea horse wanted to show her something.

A soft glow came from the end of the tunnel. As the tunnel brightened, Rani noticed that the walls glowed.

All at once, the tunnel opened up into an enormous cavern. It was so large that all of Pixie Hollow easily could have fit inside. Fingers of glittering rock dipped down from the ceiling of the cave.

"Oh, my," Rani said as she looked around.

Everywhere she turned, golden pearls like the one cradled in her arm lined the walls of the cave. The pearls reached right up to the ceiling.

"I'm the only fairy who has ever seen this," Rani said to herself.

Rani and the sea horse swam around, admiring the beautiful pearls. Finally, the sea horse looked over his shoulder at Rani.

"I hate to leave," Rani told him as they swam back through the tunnel. "It's just so beautiful here."

Rani thought he would take her back to the mermaid palace, or to the patch of seaweed where she had found him. Instead, he headed for the coral forest. "Why are we going here?" Rani wondered out loud.

The sea horse swam on. Soon, he stopped at a large cluster of seaweed. The seaweed parted and five tiny sea horses swam out, followed by another, larger sea horse. The tiny sea horses chased each other around Rani and her sea horse.

"Is this your family?" Rani asked as a tiny sea horse nibbled at her hair, then darted away. "They're so adorable!"

Rani slid off the sea horse's back and smiled at the sea horse family. They seemed so happy together. With a pang, Rani suddenly realized how much she missed her own family—the fairies.

"I wish I could go back," Rani said. "I wish I wasn't useless."

The sea horse nudged her hand.

"Thank you for showing me the lagoon," Rani told him.

Rani gave the sea horse a kiss on the snout. She waved and swam away. One of the tiny sea horses followed her for a while. But then he gave up and went back to his family.

Rani drifted, floating with the current.

She wasn't sure what to do. She didn't want to go back to the mermaids. And she felt she couldn't go back to the Home Tree. Rani sighed.

Just then, something floated down from the top of the lagoon. It was silver, and for a moment Rani thought it might be Peter Pan's mirror. But once it got closer, Rani knew what it was. It was a bubble message, like the one she had sent Tink.

A small flitterfish swam over to it. He prodded the bubble with his nose. But the bubble wouldn't burst for anyone but the person to whom it had been sent. Rani touched the bubble, and Tink's voice tumbled out.

"Oh, Rani—wherever you are—please come back!" Tink begged. "Brother Dove has been looking high and low for you. Nothing seems right without you here. We need you. Please come back. Please."

Tink must have asked another water-talent fairy to help her make the bubble message.

She must really miss me! Rani thought. *And poor Brother Dove! He's been searching all over for me.* She felt terrible that she had made her friends so unhappy.

The flitterfish swam right past Rani. "I'm glad I came to the Mermaid Lagoon," Rani said out loud. "But I think it's time for me to go home now."

10

"RANI!" FIRA CRIED as she flew over to her friend and wrapped her in a huge hug. "You're—"

"—back! I know, isn't it wonderful?" Rani asked happily.

She looked around the fairy circle, where fairies were setting up for a party. *And it's going to be in my honor!* Rani thought dizzily. The fairies were so happy that she was back that Queen Clarion had declared a holiday. All the talents were busy preparing.

There was even a water fountain. Everyone in the water talent had worked on it, including Rani. Six large spiders wove a thick curtain around the fountain so the water-talent fairies could work in secret. Pixie Hollow was buzzing with the news that Rani's party fountain was extraspecial.

I never knew that everyone cared so much, Rani thought. She stroked the soft feathers at Brother Dove's neck. He had hardly left her side since she had returned.

"Rani's back, and she's had an adventure," Tink put in.

"I know—the whole Home Tree is buzzing with the story," Fira said. "No one can wait for the big party tonight. Everyone wants to hear Rani talk about the mermaids and her trip down Havendish Stream. Did you really battle a—"

"—water snake?" Rani grinned. "I sure did."

Fira's eyes widened. "Wow. I always knew you were brave, but . . ." She shook her head.

"Well, I *was* kind of frightened," Rani admitted.

"*You* were frightened?" Tink exclaimed. "Think about how frightened we were when we couldn't find you!"

Rani frowned. "I wish I hadn't worried you. I'd fly backward if I could."

Tink grabbed her friend's hand. "I'm just glad you're home."

"I don't think any fairy has ever seen what you have, Rani," Fira said.

It was true. And while some of her adventure hadn't been much fun—like the water snake, the trip down Starfish Gap, and the mermaids, who had barely seemed to care when Rani went back to say good-bye to them—other parts, like meeting the sea horse, had been wonderful.

"Rani is special," Tink said. "There's no other fairy like her."

Just then, Vidia flew up to them. "Oh, Rani, darling, I'm so glad you're back," she said with a tight little smile. "Pet, everyone was worried *sick* about—"

"—me?" Rani said. "Don't tell me *you* were worried, Vidia."

The corners of Vidia's mouth twitched

up into an almost-smile. "Sweet child, I see we're having a little party in your honor," she said. She batted her long, dark eyelashes. "Are you going to 'help' with the fountain again?"

Tink's face turned red with anger. Rani spoke up. "Actually, Vidia, I *did* help with the fountain. Would you like to take a look?"

Without another word, Rani hopped onto Brother Dove's back. She buried her hands deep in his soft feathers and held on tightly as he took off. A moment later, she was flying through the air. The wind was cool against her face.

"Everyone, come quick!" Tink shouted. "Rani is going to unveil the fountain!" Brother Dove wheeled above the fairy circle as fairies poured into the clearing. They came from all directions. Even Queen Clarion came flying from the Home Tree. Everyone wanted to see the fountain.

Rani let Brother Dove turn twice more before she gave him the signal. With a sudden plunge, the bird dove toward the spider threads that held up the curtain. Rani pulled a small rose thorn from her hip

pocket. As Brother Dove passed the threads, she cut them one by one.

Rani broke the last thread. The curtain fluttered gently to the ground.

The fairies gasped. For a moment they were silent. Then, suddenly, they burst into applause.

The fountain was lit from the inside with a glowing golden light. The water seemed to sparkle with gold dust as it showered down the sides of the fountain. It was beautiful.

Rani and Brother Dove had spent the whole morning flying back and forth between the Mermaid Lagoon and Pixie Hollow. With the help of her sea horse friend, Rani had collected six of the magical golden Never pearls from the cave at the bottom of the lagoon and brought them back to use in the fountain. The pearls glowed just as prettily in freshwater as they did in the lagoon.

Below Rani, the fairies' applause went on and on.

Tink put her fingers into her mouth and let out a loud whistle. Showers of sparks rained from Fira's hands as she clapped. Rani blushed, but she couldn't help giggling. There was only one fairy who wasn't clapping. Vidia looked positively green.

Brother Dove fluttered his wings and landed beside Tink. Rani was instantly surrounded by fairies. Terence thumped her on the back. Tink caught Rani in a tight hug. The light-talent fairies had a million